Baba

Written and illustrated by
Ruth Brown

Andersen Press • London

We went for a walk one day, my brothers and I. Mum said we had to take our little sister with us. She's such a cry baby. She never goes anywhere without her old comfort blanket. She even talks to it, and when she's upset she hugs it and cries,

"Baba, Baba."

For Holly, Calum, Kieran and Martha

Copyright © 1997 by Ruth Brown
The rights of Ruth Brown to be identified as the author and illustrator of this work have
been asserted by her in accordance with the Copyright, Designs and Patents Act, 1988.
First published in Great Britain in 1997 by Andersen Press Ltd., 20 Vauxhall Bridge Road,
London SW1V 2SA. Published in Australia by Random House Australia Pty., 20 Alfred Street,
Milsons Point, Sydney, NSW 2061. All rights reserved. Colour separated in Switzerland by
Photolitho AG, Zürich. Printed and bound in Italy by Grafiche AZ, Verona..

10   9   8   7   6   5   4   3   2   1

British Library Cataloguing in Publication Data available.
ISBN 0 86264 730 4

This book has been printed on acid-free paper

She couldn't climb over the gate,
so she cried, "Baba, Baba."

She was frightened of the cows, so she cried, "Baba, Baba."

She couldn't cross the stream,
so she cried, "Baba, Baba."

She got caught in the brambles, so she cried, "Baba, Baba."

She even started to howl, "Baba, Baba,"
when we were just walking down the lane.
"What are you crying for now?" we shouted

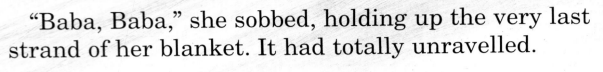

"Baba, Baba," she sobbed, holding up the very last strand of her blanket. It had totally unravelled.

"It's OK," we said. "Don't cry. We'll wind it up and then it can be knitted again. You'll see - it'll be fine."

But before we could start, our little sister pushed us out of the way.

Winding the wool, she ran up the lane,

tore through the brambles,

marched past the cows,

jumped over the stream,

and climbed the gate.

"Here you are," she said when we finally caught up with her. "Catch!"

And we played with the big
woollen ball all the way home,
my brothers, my sister and I.